happy birthday COCO

happy
birthday

Happy Birthday Coco

oneones

Kane/Miller
BOOK PUBLISHERS

Today might seem like any other day, but it's not. Today is special.

"Happy Birthday, Coco!"

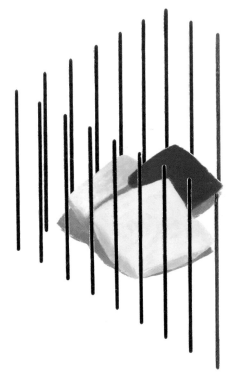

Coco…
…Was so small the first time she came home…

    …Cried during the night…

      …Chewed the table legs with her baby teeth…

        …Once climbed on to a chair and had to wait until
        someone came home to help her down…

        Today is Coco's birthday. Today, Coco is one year old.

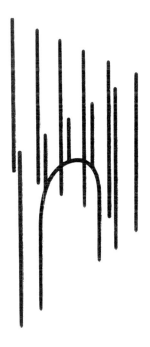

Coco's day begins like any other day.

"Good morning, Coco.

Is it time for a walk?"

Hello grass, hello ants, hello cherry tree.

The first time Coco went for a walk she tried to eat a ladybug.

When Coco was little, if she saw a big dog, she would pretend not to notice him; acting cool, she'd walk right by.

"Don't be scared, Coco. You'll be okay."

Coco has always loved tennis.

She doesn't need a racket.

Leap! Jump! Dash!

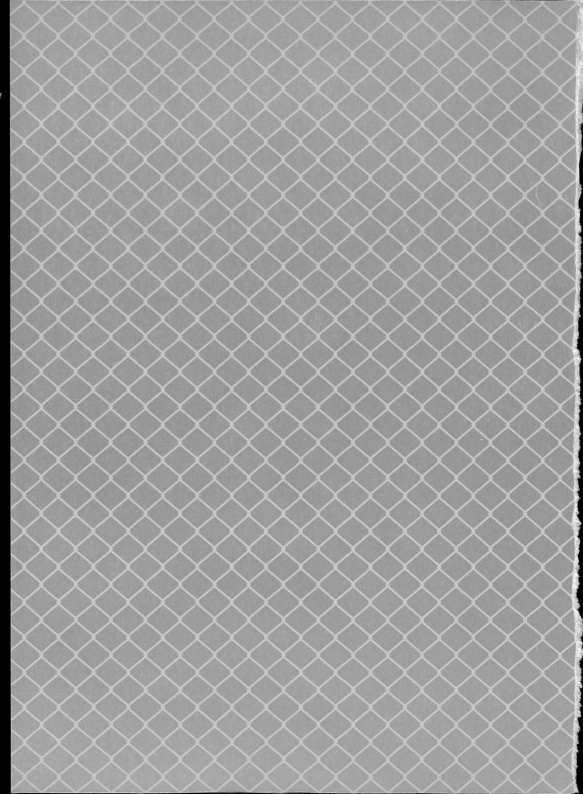

"Good job, Coco!"

Coco likes everyone.

She just wants to play, that's all.

But not everyone wants to play with her.

Wait for me, wait for me!

Maybe Coco thinks she can fly, too.

One time Coco was playing with a ball, and it landed
right in front of a very big dog.

"Be careful, Coco!"

But the big dog gently returned it.

Coco walked toward him, closer and closer.

She wasn't pretending not to notice anymore.

He's fast for such a big dog!

It was the beginning of a great friendship.

They both liked to explore.

Coco also liked to chew (mostly things she shouldn't)!

"Coco, no!"

"Bad dog, Coco!"

Shoes and toys smell the same to Coco.

She was playing. She didn't mean to be bad.

Shouting at her doesn't help.

Usually Coco loves to go for walks.

After shouting though, she just sits, and looks.

But Coco forgives easily and is soon sleeping on the bed again,
ready to be petted and loved.

No more "bad dog."

One day, Coco disappeared!

She wasn't in the house. She wasn't in the yard.

"Coco! Coco! Where are you?"

There were other dogs, but no Coco.

There she is! Finally! She's outside the vet's office.

Oh.

It's her friend.

It was time to go, but Coco wouldn't.

She wouldn't leave her friend.

Not until much, much later.

Time often makes things better.

Coco opens presents, too.

There's snow! Snow!

Coco is the first one out! It's soft, fluffy...and cold!

"Coco, look at that cloud! It looks like your old friend, doesn't it?"
The vet's was the last place we saw him.

But Coco still sits and waits for him,
even though she can't find his scent any longer.

Maybe we'll see the cloud again sometime.

Dog spelled backwards is...

Hello grass, hello ants, hello cherry tree.

The first time Coco went for a walk she tried to eat a ladybug.

Tonight might seem like any other night, but it's not.
Tonight is special.

"Happy Birthday, Coco!"

Every day is a new adventure.
Walking along the path, gazing at the cherry tree,
running through the snow.

And making friends.

Today is Coco's birthday.
Today, Coco is two years old.

"Good night, Coco. Sweet dreams."

Coco will have many more sweet dreams, many more friends,
and many more happy birthdays.

ONEONES ... is Hitomi Sago, a graphic designer, Tatsuro Kiuchi, an illustrator, and Shoko Nagamatsu, a copywriter. oneones create novelty books which people of all ages can enjoy and give to someone special.

HITOMI SAGO...
Studied fine arts at Tokyo National University of Fine Arts and Music. Working in graphic design, she has won the Rookie of the Year Award of JAGDA, the silver prize of New York ADC award, and the Minister Award of Transport and Industry Ministry for the Japan Calendar exhibition.

TATSURO KIUCHI...
Studied biology at International Christian University (Tokyo). After graduation, he studied at the Art Center College of Design in USA. He illustrates picture books, book covers, magazines, and advertisements in Japan and the rest of the world.

SHOKO NAGAMATSU...
Studied Trade and Business at Waseda University (Tokyo). She is a freelance copywriter who has won both the Asahi Advertisement Award and the Rookie of the Year Award of TCC.

Special thanks to Y.Yuko and COCO

First American Edition 2006
by Kane/Miller Book Publishers, Inc.
La Jolla, California

Copyright © 2005 by oneones
First published in Japan in 2005 under the title "HAPPY BIRTHDAY, COCO"
by Poplar Publishing Co., Ltd.
English translation rights arranged with Poplar Publishing Co., Ltd.
through Japan Foreign-Rights Centre

Library of Congress Control Number: 2006921880
Printed and bound in China
1 2 3 4 5 6 7 8 9 10

ISBN-13: 978-1-933605-13-5
ISBN-10: 1-933605-13-8